Oscar
The Mighty Crab

To Liam,
Remember you
are special.
God bless you!
Penny

OSCAR
THE MIGHTY CRAB

PENNY HIGGINS

Penny Higgins

ReadersMagnet, LLC

We are the mighty Dungeness,
we are the finest crab.

We eat small fish and worms and stuff,
whatever we can grab.

So people call us scavengers,
and maybe they're correct.

A scavenger hunt can be quite fun,
if we can just collect!

Crabs might live in the ocean
deep, out in the briny sea,

But I live in the dingy
bay with my family.

I have a happy family;
I have a dad and mom,

And several hundred kin folk,
and my best friend, Crusty Tom.

Tom calls me Mighty Oscar,
though I really am quite small.

He teases that I'm like a yoyo,
or a bouncing ball.

We are neighbors in the bay,
we have a lot of fun.

But it is gloomy night and day,
there is no moon or sun!

The murky water in the bay
is very dark and drab.

It's good for most crustaceans,
but NOT for Oscar Crab.

However, several times a week
I have a special joy,

A kind of carnival comes to humor
each crab girl and boy!

The first we know about the
rides is when the operator

Sends us down some riding
cars, like an elevator.

They're very cozy and provide
dinner and desert,

And then this fabulous fast ride
which doesn't ever hurt.

Next we see these human beings,
funny looking things

Who look at us and say, "Too small!"
and give us hearty flings

Back out into the water where
our families reside.

What makes my life worth living
is this monumental ride!

And though we only see a glimpse
of surface happenings,

We quickly get in line to see just
what the next ride brings.

Then up and down as many times
as possibly we're able

We climb into the waiting cars
and sit up to the table.

We dine on scrumptious seafood
which some very careful hand

So thoughtfully deposited
upon the bottom sand.

Oh life is boring as can be, we
have no swings or slides.

What makes my life worth living are
the great amusement rides.

But I have seen a few large friends
who happily have cheered

When entering the offered car,
but then have disappeared

Not ever to come into view by
friends or family dear.

Do they prefer to be up there?
Do they miss us here?

I have often wondered if I too
might have a chance

To see more of the upper world
than just a tiny glance.

But Crusty Tom has told me
I had better just be glad

They throw me back into the bay
to be with Mom and Dad.

Tom said I should be happy and
my life should not rotate

On carnivals and free seafood,
and other luscious bait.

Friend Tom is big, and he is wise,
and maybe he is right.

I guess I will be happy here, at
least for one more night.

10620 Treena Street, Suite 230
San Diego, California,
CA 92131 USA
www.readersmagnet.com
1.619.354.2643